D1505859

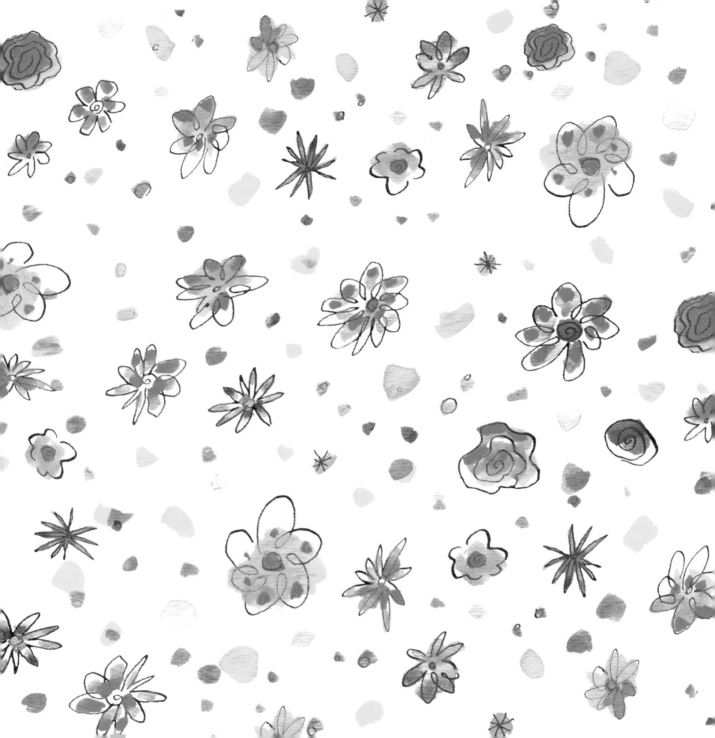

Wings of EPOH

by

GERDA WEISSMANN KLEIN

art by PETER H. REYNOLDS

First edition 2008

ISBN 978-1-891405-49-5

1 3 5 7 9 10 8 6 4 2

Book design by Martha Abdella

Printed in Cottage Grove, Minnesota
by MGB Printing Services, Inc.

Published by FableVision, Inc.
www.fablevision.com

www.autismcenter.org

This book is dedicated to everyone who
is touched by autism spectrum disorders and on a journey of hope.

Matthew was running. He was running very fast, skipping over the bright green grass, over the yellow dandelions and the smiling daisies, with the wind singing in his hair.

He felt as if he had sprouted wings. He was running without effort, skimming over the sunny meadow, alive with flowers, soft as a carpet under his nimble feet that seemed to touch down only occasionally.

Down a small hill he flew, feeling as if he could nearly lift off the ground. But as he came to the bottom, he slipped and fell with a splash at the edge of a pond.

He tried to get up, but found he couldn't. The water had seeped through the grass, and it felt warm and muddy. He lifted his foot with difficulty; clumps of grass and mud stuck to his arms and legs, which were growing heavier by the minute. It was now oppressively hot, sapping his strength. It was so dark, the sun seemed to have vanished.

Slowly he opened his eyes. It was still dark. He blinked his eyelids several times, groping around. Only now, the pond was gone. He was not

lying on grass, but sitting in his bed, curled up into a ball. He knew he was back in the real world, as he covered his ears to shield them from the loud music booming down the hall. He realized he had been dreaming, as he often did. The bright meadow over which he had danced with such ease and the fresh breeze in his hair as he was running had only existed in his mind. In truth, he could barely stand to be outside when the sun was too bright and the noises too harsh.

Just then, something gently brushed his face. What was it? Was it the breeze from the window with the billowing curtains? He looked up toward the open window and saw the dark blue sky that glittered with millions of diamond stars. They looked as though they were displayed in an enormous velvet jewel box, over which hung a round, golden moon. The stars sparkled mysteriously, as if blinking to him alone.

Matthew smiled his sweet and gentle smile. He felt a little better now, uncovered his ears and wandered around the room. Over on the

other wall, from their perch on the shelf, his toy soldiers
sat upright, their eyes wide open. Somehow, they never seemed
to need any sleep. On the other hand, his collection of bears
was always sleepy, never waking from their hibernation as they
lay scattered over the chair by his bed.

"Hey, you sleepy heads," he thought in his own special
language, tousling his favorite teddy bear's ears. "Time to get up!"

Although Matthew could talk, communication had always been

difficult for him. Often people just didn't seem to understand him.

He remembered the small box of candy hidden in his desk, a treat that his parents had given him for all his hard work. He reached behind all the papers and found it. He suddenly felt compelled to eat every piece inside it. As he devoured the last

jellybean, he felt nauseous. "Why do I always seem to eat things that make me sick?" he wondered. But he was determined not to let it get him down. No, he had always been cheerful and did his best to keep going, no matter what.

But sometimes, when he was alone and no one seemed to understand him, he did cry a little into his pillow. But then he would dry his tears and think to himself, "I am lucky—I have parents who love me a lot, and a home where I am safe... even though I still have autism."

Just what is autism? He certainly couldn't explain it. All he knew was that it made his life difficult, very difficult. He couldn't seem to make others understand him. He couldn't tell them why the sun hurt

his eyes or why loud noises made his head pound. It was times like this when he just wished he could find the words so others would understand what he was experiencing and how he was feeling.

Deep down, he knew his family loved him a lot, and they often said things to try and comfort him. But they also seemed to live in a different world than he did. His few friends didn't really understand him either, patient as they were. His toy soldiers were not much help. What about Brumas, the red bear? Although Matthew loved him best of all his toys, even Brumas didn't understand him. Every time Matthew tried to talk to him, the bear would nod his head, only to fall asleep soon after that.

Matthew picked up the little bear and cuddled him, and the bear fell asleep once more. Brumas' nodding and dreaming was infectious. Matthew closed his eyes too, feeling drowsy.

Then he blinked and he saw a movement. "Now, what was that?" he thought.

Did the model airplane on his night table move? He looked again, and saw something else. It was a butterfly! "Of all things—how wonderful," he thought.

"How nice to meet you," he silently addressed the head between those gossamer wings. "I'm so glad to have some company."

The creature seemed to understand him perfectly, even though Matthew was really only communicating with his eyes. When the butterfly replied, she had a high-pitched, silvery voice that sounded surprisingly melodious, much like a choir of silvery bells. "Nice to meet you. What a handsome little boy you are."

Matthew remembered what his mom and therapists had so patiently taught him. "Thank you," he said, remembering those two important words.

"It must be hard for you to feel so alone," the butterfly continued. "I certainly know what it means to be lonely."

"You do?" Matthew continued to speak with his thoughts. "You must have many friends, and you can fly wherever you want; everybody must admire you, and your family must love you very much."

"Well, Matthew, you only see what's on the surface." How strange that the butterfly knew his name, Matthew thought. And even stranger that the butterfly seemed to understand everything he wanted to say, even though others could not.

"People only see what they want to see," the butterfly explained. "My four wings are indeed bright and colorful on one side, but you'll find that the other side is really quite plain." Here the butterfly flipped over, and Matthew saw that the side that showed now was quite pale and ordinary.

"I think you're beautiful from every side," Matthew thought, "and the pale part of your wings looks like soft, creamy velvet."

"I'm glad you think so, but most

people who see my plain side don't bother with me at all. They think I'm dull and colorless."

"And that's how it is with me," Matthew replied.

"I know," the butterfly said in her comforting way. "Those people who only see you as someone with autism may never know the other side of you. They will neither understand nor appreciate the brilliance locked inside you. Nor will they ever see how well you add, subtract, multiply and divide, or how beautifully you play the piano."

"Oh, you do understand then!" Matthew smiled. "How can you read my mind, you who have always been so beautiful?"

"Beautiful?" the butterfly laughed. "Not always. There was never a creature uglier than I. You should have seen me when I was fat and hairy, then later when I turned bald."

"You... ugly?" Matthew asked, looking puzzled. "Some people think I am ugly because I'm different. Some kids laugh

at me and call me names. They don't understand how much it hurts me. Of course, my family—and some of my very special friends— understand and help me."

"Then you're very lucky indeed, because when I went through my most difficult moments, I had neither parents nor anybody else who cared."

"Please tell me your story," Matthew pleaded silently.

"Well, I was born like all butterflies. My mother left her eggs on the underside of the leaves on a mulberry tree. When I hatched, I was

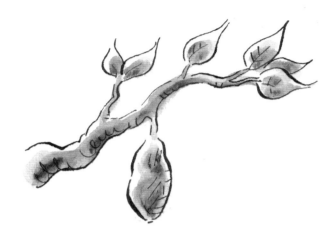

a tiny caterpillar and never knew my mother. All I knew was that I was terribly hungry and so I started to eat right away. And I ate and ate, and I grew and grew. I had many short legs but still moved very slowly, and I was very, very fat. One child saw me and called out, 'Look at that green hot dog!'"

"But what is your real name?" Matthew wondered.

"My name is Epoh," the butterfly answered.

"Epoh? I've never heard a name like that—but I think it's very nice."

"Thank you Matthew. Meanwhile, I grew bigger and bigger, and soon everybody made fun of me. At first, I had a lot of hair and then

when I turned bald and ugly,
they called me 'monster.' There was really
no end to this name-calling. I wondered if I would
ever please anyone. What would become of me? I couldn't
even tell anybody that in my fat body I had honey glands, and the
birds would have eaten me for sure if they realized how sweet I was.
That was at least one good thing about being misunderstood. But, for
everything else, I just couldn't win." Matthew nodded. He understood.

"And then, one day, I felt my skin turning hard and rigid until it
became like a suit of armor. I imagine that's what prison must be like.
You see, I couldn't move at all inside there."

"That's exactly how I feel sometimes when others can't understand me," Matthew replied. "That's when I do things to protect
myself. What happened next?"

"Well, my world was closing in on me. I was growing
more rigid, and this cruel armor was crushing me,
enveloping me and sealing me in. The darkness finally
reached my head and went over it. I thought
this was the end for me."

Matthew sat up straighter as he listened intently.

"But that was not the end; in fact, it was a new beginning. Although I could not see, I could think and feel. And I thought a lot about the world outside. I especially remembered the sunshine—how bright and warm and golden it was, brighter still in my memory. I thought of the songs of the birds, the rustling of leaves in the wind, the smell of flowers, the cool refreshing wetness of the rain. I even remembered my slow, ungainly gait while waddling from leaf to leaf with longing.

"Naturally, I couldn't tell day from night in that darkness, nor the passing of seasons, for I had lost count of time. Would I stay in this place forever or would I be released? I was very lonely and sad. Yes, I felt sorry for myself, and I must admit, I was very envious of anybody who was not in my situation. The only thing left was my memory.

"I was hanging upside down in my little cocoon for a very long time. But then I began to feel that some changes were taking place inside of me. My body was getting softer, and was pulling away from the crust, changing into something I didn't understand.

"One day, there was a tremendous crash, and I realized it was the crust breaking off my cocoon. I saw a shaft of sunlight enter my world. Soon, I was bathed in light! Even while I lived in darkness, light was my most precious memory. I thought that at least I was fortunate to have known light and all the wondrous things it can do. I had that memory. Now, here I was, exposed to sunlight once again, but feeling sticky like glue."

"That's just the way I felt in my dream," Matthew thought.

"The sun started drying me. My eyes felt strange. Did you know that each of my eyes has as many as twenty-thousand separate little eyes? I could see many things, including something quite amazing. I could see that I had begun to move, to spread my—yes, my wings. I was a butterfly! I, the tiny egg, the fat, bald, ugly caterpillar, had become a butterfly. And that dark, hard chrysalis that I had considered a prison had actually protected me from harm while I was soft and vulnerable. It had helped me change into something new, even though it was the same old me inside."

"What a beautiful story." Matthew thought. "But how did you hang on during those dark days, without losing hope?"

"That's it, Matthew—you just mentioned my name."

"Your name? But you said your name is…"

"Yes, Epoh—but you see, I spent most of my life hanging upside down, doing everything backward, or so it seemed. Read my name backward and you'll see that EPOH spells HOPE."

Matthew smiled. "I see it now!"

"But look out your window. Dawn is breaking against a rosy sky. It's the beginning of a new day, and I must fly back to my flowers and get some work done."

"Wait—don't go yet, please, don't go," Matthew's eyes pleaded with the butterfly.

"But I must. There is so much to do before…"

"Before what?"

The butterfly laughed like silver bells. "I don't really know, but each phase of my life has been more beautiful and more free than the one before. You have a loving family and friends to help you—and as long as you never lose hope, I'll be with you too."

The butterfly flew toward him, and he felt the soft wings brushing his cheek with a gentle kiss before flying out the window.

The morning was bright and fragrant. Matthew's mother walked into the room. "Good morning, Matt. How are you?"

Matthew looked up at his mother, smiled his brightest smile, and

stretched out his arms. His mom knew this was a good moment.

"Oh, look here, what's that yellow dust on your cheek?" His mother asked, reaching to brush it away,

"No," Matthew held up his hands, "it's a kiss from Epoh!"

"Epoh? Who is that?" his mother asked.

Matthew did not respond, but around his lips played a mysterious smile. He knew that his own journey, as mysterious as the butterfly's, would be just as beautiful. He was sure of it.

A Note *from* Gerda

My life and the lives of Matthew and the butterfly named Epoh
have much in common. We have found ourselves in a world where we've struggled to
communicate our thoughts, find comfort, and connect with those we love. My own life
evolved into Epoh not only because so much of it read backward, but also because its
essence has been about *hope*.

    I dedicate this book with love to Matthew and all like him who I pray will sprout
their joyous wings.

Gerda W. Klein

About *the* Author

Gerda Weissmann Klein is a well-known author, lecturer and Holocaust
survivor whose story was made into the film, *One Survivor Remembers,*
which won an Academy Award. Her books include her autobiography,
All But My Life, in print for 50 years, and *The Hours After: Letters of Love
and Longing,* which she co-authored with her late husband, Kurt. Thirty
years ago, Gerda wrote *The Blue Rose,* a touching portrayal of the uniqueness and fragility of
a young developmentally disabled girl named Jenny. *Wings of Epoh* complements the mission
of *The Blue Rose* to advance tolerance, understanding and acceptance of individuals with
differences. In that spirit, Gerda is collaborating with the Arizona-based Southwest Autism
Research & Resource Center (SARRC) in the publication and distribution of *Wings of Epoh*
and the accompanying film.

A Note *from* Peter

It was truly an honor when I was approached to help Gerda Klein bring her manuscript *Epoh* to life as a book and film. The mission of my company FableVision is to help *all* learners reach their full potential. That requires taking the time to discover each individual's strengths and capabilities. So this collaboration with Gerda has been a wonderful and natural extension of my work.

Wings of Epoh is a poetic ode to hope and human resilience. It is *my* hope that the film and book will provide encouragement for those individuals, families, schools and communities who are dealing with the unique and sometimes daunting challenges of autism spectrum disorders. This story reminds us all that hope is a powerful and enduring gift that keeps us moving forward toward a better day.

Peter H. Reynolds

About *the* Illustrator

Peter H. Reynolds is the author-illustrator of many books for children, including *The North Star, The Dot,* and *Ish,* as well as the illustrator of the popular *Judy Moody* series. He is also a passionate advocate for the non-traditional learner and is the founder of FableVision (www.fablevision.com), an educational media company that makes and distributes books, films and software. While reading Gerda's story, Peter felt a deep connection with Matthew's journey to navigate his own unique path.

Funding provided by the Scott & Ashley Coles Charitable Foundation and SARRC.

Southwest Autism Research & Resource Center

The Southwest Autism Research & Resource Center (SARRC) is a nonprofit, community-based organization in Phoenix, Arizona, dedicated to providing research, education and resources for individuals with autism spectrum disorders (ASDs) and their families. SARRC undertakes self-directed research, serves as a satellite site for national and international projects, and provides up-to-date information, training and assistance to families and professionals about autism (www.autismcenter.org). SARRC retains a portion of the proceeds from the sale of this book.

This publication is part of SARRC's Kemper & Ethel Marley Foundation Arts & Culture Program for Exceptional Children.

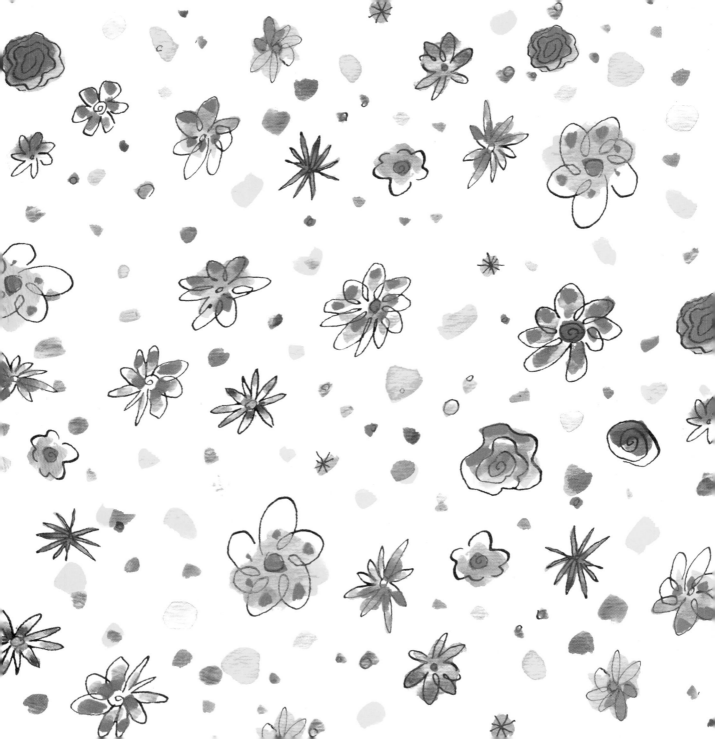